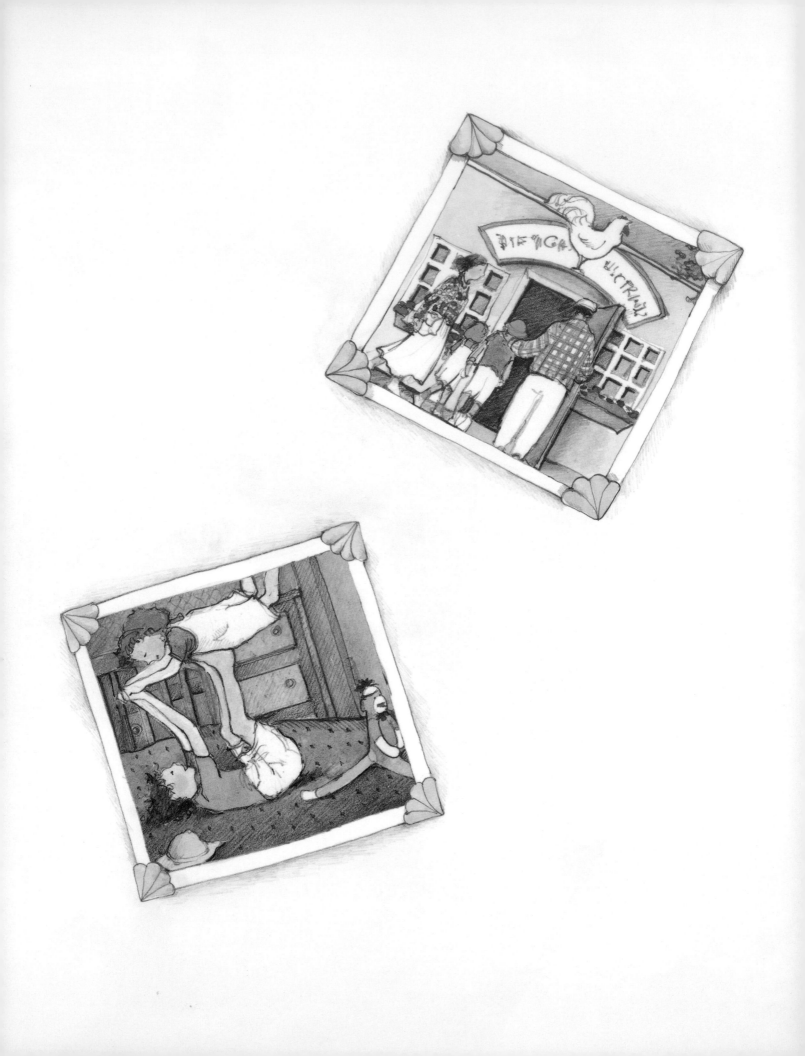

The Visit

REEVE LINDBERGH

pictures by

WENDY ANDERSON HALPERIN

DIAL BOOKS FOR YOUNG READERS NEW YORK

Tall sister, small sister, leaving together.
Aunt Laura says, "Looks like fair weather!"

Uncle Ted's truck smells of haystacks and leather.
Tall sister, small sister, leaving together.

Highway and country lane, dirt road and dust,
Beth watches leaves whirling up in a gust.

Jill sees a mailbox covered with rust.

Highway and country lane, dirt road and dust.

Porch steps and railings, front door and back.
Beth calls, "Come on! It's time to unpack!"

Uncle Ted says, "I think Jill needs a snack."
Porch steps and railings, front door and back.

Warm bread and butter, cold milk and cheese.
Slow-pouring honey from Aunt Laura's bees.

"More bread?" asks Uncle Ted. Jill says, "Yes, please!"
Warm bread and butter, cold milk and cheese.

Closets and cupboards, places to hide.
Beth says, "Let's change first, then go outside."

Jill looks around with eyes open wide.
Closets and cupboards, places to hide.

Hay barn and carriage barn, horse stable, stall.
Beth climbs up high and looks out over all.

Jill finds a nest in a hole in the wall.

Hay barn and carriage barn, horse stable, stall.

Maple tree, willow tree, poplar and pine.
Beth watches swallows, swooping to dine.

Jill finds a lost kite, tangled in twine.

Maple tree, willow tree, poplar and pine.

Wild iris, pink lilac, peony, rose.
Beth holds a blossom up to Jill's nose.

Jill sees a hummingbird next to the hose.

Wild iris, pink lilac, peony, rose.

Kitchen clock, mantel clock, dinner bell's chime.
Aunt Laura on the porch: "Girls! Supper time!"

Hand in hand, up the hill, Beth and Jill climb.
Kitchen clock, mantel clock, dinner bell's chime.

Chicken and biscuits, strawberry pie.
Uncle Ted heaps the plates higher than high.

Beth starts to yawn, Jill is closing one eye.
Chicken and biscuits, blueberry pie.

Tall shadows, dark corners, noises at night.
Uncle Ted asks, "Will you girls be all right?"

Aunt Laura tells them she'll leave on one light.
Tall shadows, dark corners, noises at night.

Comforter, pillow, blanket and bear.
Jill wishes Mama and Daddy were there.

Beth says, "My bed's too big—why don't we share?"
Comforter, pillow, blanket and bear.

Moonlight and lightning, fireflies and stars.
Beth hears a freight train with rumbling cars.

Jill hears a thrush singing—just a few bars!
Moonlight and lightning, fireflies and stars.

Windowpane, skylight, dormer and bay.
Light muslin curtains that rustle and sway.

Sisters asleep and dreaming till day.
Windowpane, skylight, dormer and bay.

Tall sister, small sister, yawning and waking.
Sun streaming in, biscuits are baking.

Tall sister, small sister, a new day is breaking
with fun, adventure . . . and memory-making.

Published by Dial Books for Young Readers
A division of Penguin Young Readers Group
345 Hudson Street, New York, New York 10014
Text copyright © 2005 by Reeve Lindbergh
Pictures copyright © 2005 by Wendy Anderson Halperin
All rights reserved
Manufactured in China on acid-free paper
1 3 5 7 9 10 8 6 4 2

Library of Congress Cataloging-in-Publication Data
Lindbergh, Reeve.
The visit / Reeve Lindbergh ;
pictures by Wendy Anderson Halperin.
p.   cm.
Summary: Two sisters share an experience of country life
when they visit their aunt and uncle.
ISBN 0-8037-1189-1
[1. Sisters—Fiction. 2. Country life—Fiction.
3. Stories in rhyme.] I. Halperin, Wendy Anderson, ill. II. Title.
PZ8.3.L6148 Vk 2005   [E]   dc21   2002013245

The art was created using pencil and watercolor.